ADOPTED
by the EAGLES

Paul Goble has written and
illustrated these books:

Custer's Last Battle
The Fetterman Fight
Lone Bull's Horse Raid
The Friendly Wolf
The Girl Who Loved Wild Horses
The Gift of the Sacred Dog
Star Boy
Buffalo Woman
The Great Race
Death of the Iron Horse
Her Seven Brothers
Beyond the Ridge
Dream Wolf
I Sing for the Animals
Crow Chief
Love Flute
The Lost Children

—and the books about Iktomi:

Iktomi and the Boulder
Iktomi and the Berries
Iktomi and the Ducks
Iktomi and the Buffalo Skull
Iktomi and the Buzzard

ADOPTED
by the EAGLES

a Plains Indian story
of friendship and treachery
told & illustrated
by Paul Goble

Bradbury Press · New York

Maxwell Macmillan Canada · Toronto
Maxwell Macmillan International
New York · Oxford · Singapore · Sydney

Bradbury Press
Macmillan Publishing Company
866 Third Avenue
New York, NY 10022

Maxwell Macmillan Canada, Inc.
1200 Eglinton Avenue East
Suite 200
Don Mills, Ontario M3C 3N1

Macmillan Publishing Company is part of the Maxwell Communication Group of Companies.

First edition
Printed in the United States of America on recycled paper
10 9 8 7 6 5 4 3 2 1

Library of Congress Cataloging-in-Publication Data
Goble, Paul.   Adopted by the eagles / story and illustrations by Paul Goble.—1st ed.   p.   cm.
Includes bibliographical references.   Summary: Two friends go out hunting for horses—but only one returns—in this story based in the Lakota Indian tradition.   ISBN 0-02-736575-1.   1. Dakota Indians—Legends. [1. Dakota Indians—Legends.   2. Indians of North America—Legends.]
I. Title.   E99.D1G577   1994   398.2′089975—dc20   [E]   93-24047

The text of this book is set in Caslon #540.

The illustrations are in India ink and watercolor, on Oram and Robinson Limited, Waltham Cross, England, watercolor boards, reproduced in combined line and halftone.
Book design by Paul Goble

Several steps were taken to make this an environmentally friendly book. The paper is made from not less than 50 percent recycled fibers. The inks used are soy based. Finally, the binders board is 100 percent recycled material.

REFERENCES: Chief Luther Standing Bear, *Stories of the Sioux* ("The Hunter Who Was Saved by Eagles," p. 20), Houghton Mifflin, Boston, 1934 (republished by University of Nebraska Press, Lincoln, 1988); Richard Erdoes, *The Sound of Flutes—and Other Indian Stories* ("Spotted Eagle and Black Crow," told by Jenny Leading Cloud, p. 25), Pantheon Books, New York, 1976; Gerald and Vivian One Feather, *Ekanni Ohunkakan* ("The Two Cousins and the Two Eagles," told by Edgar Red Cloud, p. 161), Oglala Sioux Culture Center, Red Cloud Indian School, Pine Ridge, 1974; R. D. Theisz, *Buckskin Tokens—Contemporary Oral Narratives of the Lakota* (told by Henry Black Elk, p. 19), Sinte Gleska College, Rosebud, 1975.

THANK YOU: Lydia Whirlwind Soldier, Indian Studies Curriculum Specialist for Todd County School District, South Dakota, for your cultural and linguistic help.

THANK YOU: Jim Little Wounded (Prairie Edge, Rapid City, South Dakota) for making the beaded memorial frame shown on the next page.

Ehanni iyayapi ki, wichunkiksuya pi.
I have made this book remembering
Chief Edgar Red Cloud, 1896–1977.
He gave me a Lakota name, and called me "Son."
Woplia ate.

I also dedicate this book to my wife, Janet,
and our son, Robert, with much love.

Friends playing a game called *pte heste*, "buffalo
horn tips." Arrows with heavy polished buffalo
horn tips are thrown underhand along the ice.
The arrow must strike the ground between two
markers, and the arrow which slides the farthest
wins.

Eagle's wingbone whistle, used in certain
ceremonies, and also blown when a person is
sad or in difficulties, to call upon the strength
and inspiration of the Eagle. Given by Edgar.

Chief Edgar Red Cloud

1896–1977

AUTHOR'S NOTE:

There are two main ideas inside this Lakota story which appear often in North American Indian literature: treachery between two warriors or hunters when they are far from home, and animals or birds who help people in need. Both were surely familiar ideas to our Stone Age ancestors all over the earth.

This book is based on a more complex story which is said to have been a favorite of Chief Red Cloud (1822–1909), *Mahpiya Luta*, the warrior leader of the Ogalalas who won the Powder River War of 1866–1868. He told the story to his great-grandson, Edgar Red Cloud (1896–1977); see photograph, opposite page. Edgar was a well-known storyteller at Pine Ridge, South Dakota, and one of the last in the truly ancient oral tradition, before reading and writing, and television, brought irrevocable changes. He had the gift to take you right into the story he told. He did not use a lot of words, or give detailed descriptions, but sketched the picture quite slowly with evocative and powerful words, leaving his listeners to complete the picture in the way each wanted to imagine it. It was a joy to listen to his slow speech, the way he lengthened some vowels, and his frequent repetitions for emphasis, even his silences. Perhaps most wonderful of all were his facial expressions, gentle manner, and his veritable dictionary of slow hand and arm and body gestures, because he spoke while using a form of the old universal Indian sign language which Indian people used during Buffalo Days.

I like to think that Edgar somehow sensed, right from the start (1959), that I would one day make books of some of the stories he told me. At first I had no idea that I would ever write! Myths and legends did not much interest me; I thought they were mere fantasy. I used to wish he would tell ''real'' stories about his great-grandfather's bravery against the soldiers. Later, after he had gone ''beyond the ridge,'' I understood that he had been telling me stories which help to bring sacred thoughts and truths into clearer focus, like traditional myths the world over. God and the Great Spirit are one. The myths were his scriptures.

Finally, it needs to be stated that the traditional *kola* friendship of two Lakota men, as described in this story, was never a homosexual relationship. *Kolas* sought to guard each other from all errors; to share their strengths while walking life's Good Red Road together.

A NOTE FOR TEACHERS:

When a book like this has been read in the classroom, students are sometimes asked to write their own ''Indian'' stories. It is not asked with bad intentions, but it belittles these traditional stories, suggesting that any child can invent them. When studying the Greek myths, or the legends of King Arthur, or Bible stories, students would never be asked to invent stories in the manner of . . . Instead, children should be encouraged to write down the stories in their own words to help remember them. Over the years they will come to think about the inner meanings which all these stories hold.

*D*uring the old Buffalo Days two young men sometimes formed a special friendship. They became **kolas**, friends. Kolas swore to do everything together, to look after each other's family, to help each other hunt, to share everything to the last morsel of food; and, if it had to be, even to die in the defense of his friend. They tried to keep the Four Virtues in their thoughts: Bravery,[1] Patience,[2] Kindness,[3] and Wisdom.[4] Being kolas was a difficult, and sacred relationship.

There were two young men, called White Hawk and Tall Bear, **Chetan Sa** and **Mato Hanska**. They were **kolas**, friends.

1. *Woohitika*
2. *Wowachintanka*
3. *Wachantognaka*
4. *Woksape*

Everyone loved and admired White Hawk and Tall Bear. People noticed that they both liked to be with the beautiful Red Leaf, **Wahpe Lutawin**, and they would often see the three together, dressed in their finest clothes, riding around the tipi circle.

The women shook their heads, saying: "Red Leaf cannot marry both of them; how will she ever choose?" But the men answered: "Red Leaf will know. Tall Bear and White Hawk are still young, and there is no hurry. They are kolas."

And all this was true.

One day White Hawk said to Tall Bear: "Friend, last night while I slept I had a good dream: I dreamed that we captured horses from our enemies. I saw we had many, many beautiful horses and they were of every color! It's true! In my dream I could hear people cheering us! It's surely a good sign. Let's go, just you and me together. Let's bring all those horses home!"

Tall Bear replied: "Yes! Let's go. You are my kola. Whatever you want to do, I want to do it with you."

They left on foot so that they would be able to hide when in the country of their enemies. Each carried his blanket, bow and arrows, spare moccasins, and a little dried meat. Tied around his waist each had several light buffalo-hair ropes, to lead home the horses which he hoped to capture.

At first they travelled during the day, but when they reached enemy country they walked only at night so that they would not be seen. At dawn they looked for a place to hide and to sleep during daylight.

Night after night they walked, but they could not find the camp and the horse herds of their enemies. There was not a sign of them anywhere. Disappointed, and hungry, and very tired with walking so far, they turned back towards home.

For one last look out over the surrounding country, they climbed a lonely high butte, hoping to discover smoke rising from the enemy campfires.

Standing on the topmost rocks above the pine trees, the whole earth was spread out below them, and yet there was not a sign of a camp or horse herds anywhere.

They saw a nest with
two young eagles on a
rocky ledge below them.
"Kola," said White
Hawk, "instead of going
home without anything,
let's take these young
eagles back. They'll give
us feathers from time to
time."

"Yes," Tall Bear
agreed. "Everyone
wants to wear sacred
eagle feathers."

"Then let's tie our
ropes together," White
Hawk suggested. "I'll
hold the rope. You go
down. Tie up the eagles,
and I'll haul them up
one at a time."

They agreed on this
plan. Tall Bear let himself
down, slowly, so that he
did not frighten the
young eagles.

Just as Tall Bear reached the pile of sticks which was the nest, his friend jerked the rope out of his hands and pulled it up out of reach.

"Kola!" he called up. "What happened? How will I get back up again?" There was no answer.

"Kola!" he called again. "Help me!"

White Hawk looked down from the top. "Help yourself!" he replied.

"Don't leave me, friend!" called out Tall Bear. "Help me, kola!" He listened ...
but only the echoes answered him:
"Help me, kola!"

His friend had left him on that narrow ledge, to starve, and to fall to an awful death on the rocks far below.

Tall Bear crouched at one side of the nest; at the other side the two young eagles hissed and screeched at him. Any moment their parents would return and attack him. The sun went behind the cliff. A wind gathered the clouds, and it grew cold. He cried, thinking of his mother and father, and Red Leaf, whom he would never see again.

Suddenly it came to him: "That's why he left me here to die! He wants Red Leaf for himself! **Ho Wakan Tanka, onshimala ye**! Great Spirit, have pity on me! Have pity on me!" he asked again and again.

Soon he felt stronger; the Great Spirit would help him.

Tall Bear did not die. The young eagles made him their brother; they shared the nest with him, and the parents adopted him for their son. They brought him meat, and so he lived.

The day came when the young eagles had grown their feathers, and they wanted to fly from the nest.

Tall Bear prayed: "Have pity on me! **Wani wachin!** I want to live!" He quickly seized both eagles by the legs, one in each hand, closed his eyes, and leaped away from the ledge, far out over the abyss.

His Eagle brothers
carried him to earth.

Tall Bear thanked the eagles: "My brothers, you have saved my life. When the leaves fall I will bring you gifts." By the time he reached home again, he was tired and hungry, and his clothes were tattered.

Everyone was excited to see him; they thought he was dead because White Hawk had told them that his kola had been killed by the enemy.

When Tall Bear returned, White Hawk fled from the village and was never seen again. People wanted to pursue and kill him, but Tall Bear told them not to. "He is my kola," he reminded them.

During the Falling Leaves Moon, Tall Bear and Red Leaf were married. Tall Bear told Red Leaf: "I promised my Eagle brothers I would return with gifts. Let's go together."

He stood again on top of the lonely butte, Red Leaf beside him. The nest was empty; the eagles gone. He took his pipe and offered it with outstretched arms to the sky. Turning, he gave the Eagle's cry to each of the Four Winds:
E-e-e-ya! E-e-e-ya!
E-e-e-ya! E-e-e-ya!

In a little while, up among the clouds two black specks were making circles, soaring closer, ever larger. Two magnificent young Spotted Eagles landed on the rocks close by.

Tall Bear and Red Leaf gave the Eagles dried meat mixed with berries, which is called **wasna**, and tied ribbons to their legs.

"My brothers," said Tall Bear, "I am glad we are all here today. You are wise; you see everything in the heavens and on the earth. You give your feathers for everyone to wear, and you carry our thoughts high above to the Great Spirit."
Red Leaf said: "We Two-legged People and your Eagle Nation* are relatives, always."

*A*nd so the relationship was made new again. This is the story the wise ones used to tell. **Hechetu.** That's it.

*Wanbli Oyate

Edgar Red Cloud and Paul Goble in 1959